Prayers for Ava

Izabela Bamber, Jacob Bleakley,
Pheobe Callaghan, Lois Chapman,
Jessica Ellwood, Alicia Gillon,
Anjali Mistry, Catherine Scanlan and
Scarlett Wright

with

Mr Graham

ISBN-10:154556745X
ISBN-13: 978-1545567456

DEDICATION

Thank you to our families for your love and support
through the writing of our novel and to all the teaching
staff that have worked with us at James Brindley.
Together, you have taught us to enjoy reading, writing and
expressing ourselves. And for that we are very grateful.

CONTENTS

ACKNOWLEDGMENTS

Thank you to Mr Graham and Mrs O'Neill for their assistance in proof reading and editing our work.

1

Edward sat alone in his armchair, reminiscing on his past. A World War one veteran, he was now an old pensioner living in a retirement home. He had no contact with people outside of the dull walls that stabilised the building. Every day he would sit there, in the same place, same position, looking back on his four dreadful years in the war.

There was nothing glamorous about Edward's life in the trench. They were dirty, smelly, infested with rats and riddled with diseases. Many people were diagnosed with trench foot, a nasty disease soldiers suffered when their feet experienced prolonged exposure to damp and cold conditions. Indulging in his ruminations, Edward recalled rubbing whale oil on his feet to prevent this awful disease. He, like all the men in the trenches, would also have to keep their feet as dry, warm and clean as possible. Considering they had to live in the trenches, keeping warm and clean wasn't easy. Edward was lucky not to catch this terrifying disease.

The trenches were long, narrow ditches dug into the ground, where the soldiers would spend their day and night. Some men were on duty up to twenty hours a day. The trenches smelt awful and were very unhygienic. Dead bodies lay nearby, not all were buried, and the latrines sometimes over flowed, causing the trenches to flood. Rats raided the trenches and Edward came across some that were huge! With rodents roaming the living quarters, staying healthy was very difficult.

Being on the front line was life-threatening. Every day, over ten thousand soldiers were killed. Edward didn't believe in the famous verse *Dulce et decorum est pro patria mori*. Whether it was quoted from Horace or Owen, Edward believed it to be a lie. He'd lived it. He'd breathed it. He'd witnessed compatriots and friends die before his very eyes- mown down by German gunfire, stabbed by a bayonet or drowning and writhing in agony as a result of a German chlorine gas attack. The soldiers that survived these excruciating four years of war were extremely lucky to be alive. Edward fully appreciated his luck. He'd gone to war with a heart full of hope. Like most, he'd believed it would be a short lived affair. That he'd be back in the arms of loved ones soon. That he'd have Ava back in his arms in a matter of months. He hadn't bargained on four years. No-one had. At least, no-one would admit to it. The bloodiest war on record. And he'd been part of it. *Licensed murder* was how Edward reflected on it. They were just men and he was just a humble man. Men with very little differences, trying to *make* a difference. Fighting for freedom or the hope of it.

Being on the front line meant leaving your family and all that you loved behind. Edward missed home dearly. All he wanted was to go home and live a normal life. That was all any of the soldiers wanted. To go home to their families. Unfortunately, this was not an option. They had to stay and serve for their country.

Fighting for Blighty had really changed Edward and he recognised this himself. He'd put it to the back of his mind and got on with his life as best he could, when he returned to England. But the events of seven days ago had given him all the time in the world for reflection and he realised that he was not the man he could have been.

Despite all of these gloomy thoughts, Edward fully appreciated that he was one of the lucky few. He'd survived Gallipoli and then been part of the British forces alleviating the French at Verdun. So many of his friends didn't make it. Whole families killed. Whole towns devastated, wallowing in grief for the sons who never returned. Edward had become very close with some of the other soldiers, yet few of the friendships lasted very long. The more bullets and shells rained, the more worried Edward became. All it took was one bullet. Friend after friend, before his eyes- and there was never anything he could do to save them. Of those around who survived, a handful were shot for experiencing severe psychological trauma. Shell shock. *Stir crazy,* the yanks called it. Being in the war had a huge impact on a soldier. All that death and violence drove many soldiers insane. The army couldn't afford to carry cowards or traitors either, so soldiers who tried to flee or run away would be killed at dawn by the military command. Edward's heart ached from their death. However he managed to stay strong, determined not to end up like these poor soldiers. He soon came to the conclusion that it was best to avoid investing in friendships. That emotional investment only brought heartache and pain. Instead, he'd focus on Ava. He'd pass the time dreaming of her, back home, and the future they'd have. A pencil and a notepad. His saving grace. His redemption. His only link to the outside world. Edward looked after that pencil and notepad like his very life depended on it. In many ways, it did. He'd faithfully write to Ava as often as he could. He'd tell her what it was like but spare the quite horrific details of the reality he faced every day. He'd talk of their future together and the life they would live when he returned. The family they would have and the good times ahead. And he always signed off by telling her how much he loved her; that the thought of her was the only thing that kept him going.

Even now, sat aged in his chair in the retirement home, Edward could picture her. Her beautiful curls. The tiny mole on the side of her neck. How her mouth curled like the lip of a majestic wave. Remembering her smell, he was right back there with her. For these few minutes a day, Edward the pensioner was Edward the soldier, back in the trenches remembering his love fondly. But the cruel chime of the grandfather clock in the hall brought Edward racing back to the present and brought with it a broken man. His true love seemed as far away as ever. Out of reach, in fact, for she had died just last year.

2

Ava had a range of feelings when her Dad told her they were definitely moving. The offer had been accepted. Moving town meant moving school too and, while she was excited for a fresh start, she was apprehensive whether she would fit in. Making friends wasn't exactly one of Ava's strengths.

Last week, they'd gone to view an old house that used to be a retirement home. Ava sensed something peculiar while there. There was something different about the house, however she couldn't put her finger on it. Was it the structure of the house? The smell? The old fashioned wallpaper that had faded in the sunlight and was beginning to peel off? She couldn't be sure what it was but she sensed an overwhelming sadness about the place. Old paintings and photographs hung crookedly from the walls. For a moment, she drifted away imagining the photographs and paintings hanging straight and gleaming, smiling down upon visitors. It must have been a long time ago. The dust alone told her that. One black and white photograph in particular caught her eye. An older man, his arm lovingly around a lady. She'd no idea who they were but she felt drawn to this particular picture frame.

Ten weeks later the papers were signed and Ava was about to start a whole new life.

Moving day was hard for Ava. She didn't know how to feel. Dad was busy fussing and asking her about her new room. *It's not bad, Dad.* He looked confused for a moment, before quickly realising what was going on. *Look, I know this is hard for you, but don't worry about making new friends. Your new school will be great! You'll see; you just need to give it a chance.* Ava thought for a second. *It's not that; I just have a strange feeling about this house. I don't know why. Are you sure you thought this through? Are you sure you made the right decision about moving?* He talked her through the happiness he felt when he received the job offer. *It's a fresh start for us. A chance to move on with our lives. I know things have been difficult since your Mum passed away.* Their conversation stopped as abruptly as it had started. Neither of them could speak after the mention of Mum. Anxious about her first day at school and worn out from the conversation, Ava decided to get an early night. She didn't want to be late for her first day at her new school.

The next morning, Ava woke up really early. Not just because she didn't want to be late, but because nerves had infiltrated her sleep, leaving her a semi-conscious prisoner for much of the night. Ava felt like she had nothing to wear. All of her clothes were creased from being in boxes and it turned out that her dad had forgot to pack the ironing board. So, a creased vest and denim shorts it was! Her day was already going wrong and she wasn't even at school yet. All the food was still in the boxes so all she could eat was a Granola bar. She couldn't find her purse either so she couldn't buy any lunch. At this rate, Ava was going to end up living on Granola bars!

Come on Ava, get in the car or we'll both be late for our first day! Ava grabbed her bag and ran downstairs, straight out of the front door. Before getting in the car, she took a brief moment to look at the outside of the new house. She still couldn't figure out what was different about it. But Dad was moaning about being late for his new job, so Ava climbed into the car and set off for school.

Arriving at school, she had mixed emotions about it. *Have a good first day, darling.* Ava hollered back a nervous reply as Dad sped off. As she walked into her new school, Ava noticed people glaring at her. Was it the creased vest? Was it because she was new? Deep down she was hoping that they were thinking that she was beautiful. However, she knew that the people looking at her were probably judging her harshly. She could tell that just by the way they were looking at her.

Ava's first class was history. She hated history so was not looking forward to the lesson. When she walked into the classroom, people were staring at her. She found a seat at the back and sat down whilst her teacher babbled on about Henry the eighth to the class. The rest of the day was a blur. She still had one last class left. Art. Ava enjoyed art. However, before she could start the lesson, she had to find the class! The lesson was already ten minutes old and she was none the wiser. She nearly had a mental break down.

There was only ten minutes of the lesson left when she finally found the classroom and stumbled in. She explained to the teacher that she was new and she didn't know where the class was. Fortunately the teacher accepted her seemingly lame excuse and quickly explained what she had missed. They had been talking about their new art topic-Pop Art. The teacher handed her a booklet about Pop Art before Ava made her way to the car park to meet her dad.

How was your first day, Pumpkin? Ava nodded and mumbled. It was usually Mum she'd speak to about these things. But Mum was gone. Dad was having to play at being Mum while still being Dad. Ava hadn't yet got used to it. She wondered if she ever would. *Well at least it wasn't horrible. I remember my first day at my new school; I walked into someone and dropped all my food over him in the canteen. He hated me for it. Became my nemesis. But tell me this- did you make any new friends today?"*
Ava reluctantly told him about a girl who said she'd liked her shoes. She seemed nice but she wouldn't class her as friend. *Oh well, I guess you're bound to have better luck tomorrow.*

3

Another passing year in the trenches felt like an extended sentence. For some of his comrades, it had proved to be a life sentence. Or a death sentence, in fact. Edward was still desperately fighting for his life. The great peril of twenty hour shifts had made him weak. Death had, on numerous occasions, stood immediately before him. Hell was all around him. The Great War.

Every day he longed for the love of his girlfriend's tender heart. He wanted to leave his torment behind. To propose to her. To place the ring upon her finger. The only gifts he was party to giving or receiving, however, were bandages and iodine. Not much to attend to the wounds and scars of war let alone the wounds and scars of the mind. While his soul had become the devil's playground, his angel's heart was his haven. Ava's letters fought the biggest battle of all- to keep him alive on the inside. In between the bloodshed and horror, Edward found solace in reading her words and writing back to his beloved.

My darling Ava,

It's been a long and hard journey at this time in our life however, I'm sure we will get through it. You make me stronger- a warrior in the flesh and pure in the soul. Although it has been years since I last got to experience your smile and calming voice, your letters truly speak to me. They keep me alive. You are my beating heart and I vow to return to make you my wife.

When I'm in the trench, reading your letters, I forget the inhumanity and starvation. I hunger only for you. My love for you is bursting from my soul, heart and my lungs. Letter after letter, tear after tear, smile after smile, my heart rises higher when it thinks of you and I cannot wait for the day that we are reunited. I promise we will soon be together again.

Your true love,

Edward
xx

Line after line, page after page, Edward and his trusty pencil continued to write, unaware of what the future held and the emotions that lingered at home.

Lost in thoughts of Ava, Edward momentarily drifted away, wallowing in a world of his own. As a shot resonated across the gloomy battlefield, he was suddenly back in the real world. He felt the bullet rip through his body. His body began to shut down; his eyes closed, his pulse became faint and his surroundings became a distant blur. His heart was paralysed, his true love lost in the mist of time as he fell unconscious.

Hours later, his slumbering body awakened. Bleary eyed, he stared at the pale white wall which temporarily concealed his true surroundings – an unsanitary hospital.

For a long time he questioned how he'd arrived here. The soldier in him tried to move. He was also unable to do so, however. Shifting the focus of his eyes downwards, his heart sank. There, before him, lay a swamp of blood surrounded by patches of flesh protruding from his leg. The world around him went distant again as Edward passed out.

Before long the wound had become septic, puss deriving from the bullet hole. It seemed as if the only possible option was to amputate the limb. But fate intervened and Edward was spared his leg. He would, however, no longer be able to serve in the war and was left with a limp as a reminder of his sacrifice for Blighty. Reluctantly, it was agreed that he should return home. He would be able to see his dear Ava once again

Thoughts whirred around in his head on his journey back home. How would Ava react when she saw him again? What would he say to her first? He came up with many ways to greet her when he arrived home but settled on a fresh bouquet of flowers. He wouldn't have to wait much longer. She'd be there. Right in front of him.

After what seemed like forever, he placed his steel tipped boots on the cobbled streets and, with his rucksack on his back, he made his way back to Ava's parent's home, hobbling every step of the way. His heart was filled with so much joy, excitement and anticipation as he arrived on her doorstep. It was like time had stood still. The red door. The hanging basket. The net curtains drawn.

With trepidation, he gave a friendly knock upon the door. His routine knock. He was sure Ava would recognise it. He pulled out a bouquet of sweet smelling flowers and gazed at them, lost in thought. Seconds later he was stunned to find an unfamiliar man bearing down at him from the door frame. Perplexed, all manner of thoughts flooded his conscience. Had Ava moved? Had she met someone else? Did she still love him? Had she married while he was gone? Sternly, he asked what business the stranger had being in the house.

The man stared despondently down at his feet as a familiar face appeared at the door. Ava. *Edward!* She fought back her smile. Then fought back her tears. *My sister - George's wife- died. How did...* Edward looked up slowly, trying to process what he had just been told. He embraced the man in a sympathetic hug, feeling slightly guilty for thinking such negative thoughts about a person he had just met. *Ava!* Pulling himself together again, Edward launched the flowers and his arms around Ava. He felt guilty for smiling having just heard of her sister's death but he couldn't have stopped himself if he tried. Together they made their way to the living room where Ava's father lay slumped in his armchair, sipping from a glass of whiskey to help numb his grief. Edward sat down beside Ava and placed a loving kiss on her forehead, handing her the bouquet. Out of the darkness of her personal tragedy, the light in Edward's eyes showed the way. With tears falling from her eyes, Ava closed her hand and clutched the flowers close to her heart. She gently whispered in his ear. *I've missed you, Dear.*

4

A week into her new life, Ava was still waking up with a knot in her stomach, full of trepidation. She found her escape in many of her favourite books. Dressed and ready to face the day, Ava was out of the door by half past eight and on her way to school.

The playground was always full of pupils when she got there. Tall and small. Sporty and geeky. All ready to go in and start learning. The school building towered over the playground and the bike shelters, casting a shadow in the early morning sun. A few bikes lay untidily in the shelters. The realisation that Ava still knew no one hit her. Everyone else was with *someone*. They were talking. Laughing. Pranking. But Ava was alone. Overcome with self-consciousness, she could feel herself shrinking back with herself- like a hermit crab retreating into its shell. She went in and sat down. Maths! Ava liked numbers- they never lied. They only ever told the truth. She got the whole page finished and moved up a stage in her learning. Whatever that meant. She felt the glare of the class on the back of her neck. *Who did she think she was? Showing off like that in your first fortnight. Being the teacher's pet.* She tried to ignore it but the feeling continued to linger. The last lesson before lunch was English! She stumbled around the building, desperately trying to find her next classroom. At last. A friendly face. *Are you looking for Mrs Gregson's room? It's that way.* It wasn't. In fact, it was completely the opposite direction. Ava hurried back, hoping to be on time. She didn't see the outstretched foot. She didn't have time to put her hands out in front of her. Her face hit the ground with a heavy thud. The corridor erupted in laughter. She choked back the tears and ran. She found it. Eventually.

The class had their books out and had started reading the next chapter of Z for Zachariah. Inside, Ava felt her heart skip a beat with excitement. She'd loved Robert C O'Brien's tale of Mrs Frisby. She'd felt empathy with the widowed fieldmouse. She was immediately hooked on the post apocalyptic setting. She was told to write a paragraph about her feelings on the first chapter. The teacher said they could go for dinner when the work was finished. *Ava, that is sensational. You've really understood what the author is trying to convey here.* She felt the sneers and stares burning the back of her neck again. She couldn't wait for home time.

Dinner brought no comfort. Ava had never felt so alone. She longed for her friends back home. For Jill, Katy and Sophie. The canteen was grotty and many of the teenagers were messing with their food. Her sandwich disappeared quickly. Lost in her thoughts, Ava was brought back with a splash of Coke hitting her neck. More laughter. She couldn't look. Couldn't face them. Instead, she packed up her lunch box and headed for her locker. 417. She inserted the key and opened it. A note. Inside her locker. *Sorry about before. I actually really like you. You're beautiful.* A phone number. Maybe things weren't as bad as they seemed.

Getting back into class after dinner, she sat in her science seat and got out her equipment. *I am going to bring round these new science books for you to read. Once you have your book you may start reading at page twenty.* So that's what they did for the next half an hour. Next, they had to analyse one page of their book (their choice of page). Ava chose page thirteen. Unlucky for some, thirteen just happened to be her lucky number. So that's what she did for the rest of the lesson. At last, it seemed as if things were settling down. But the final lesson of the day was P.E. Ava had been dreading it. The girls in the changing rooms. The shower cubicles. The thought of other girls seeing her changing. Waiting for the teacher to arrive, they all started to change for the lesson. The changing room was loud and intimidating. Gaggles of girls sat gossiping in little cliques around the room. And Ava. Alone, by herself. She felt that they were whispering about her. She didn't know for sure but she felt it. When the teacher arrived, they went into the hall and started the warm up: five star jumps, five squats, and ten burpees. After they had finished the warm up they got into partners and sat down. A really nice girl chose to be partners with Ava, which she really liked. The ship was slowly turning!

In the shower cubicle after the lesson, Ava reached for her

towel. Her eyes filled with water, she fumbled frantically to no avail. It was gone. She knew she'd hung it up. But it wasn't there. Panic descended over her like a mist. Wiping her eyes, she could see that her towel was on the floor on the other side of the changing room. Someone must have reached over and snatched her towel. A rotten end to a rotten day. Repeated calls for assistance went unheard. At last the teacher came to Ava's rescue, handing her the towel over the cubicle door. *A prank for the newbie, Ava. Nothing to worry about.* But Ava didn't see the funny side.

On the walk home, Ava decided that she wanted to be popular with the other girls. She yearned for a companion and didn't have many friends yet. She didn't know how to get people's attention in a positive way, didn't know what they liked or their individual personalities. Back at her old school she had many more friends than she did now because she had grown up with them. She had many ideas. Some were better than others. She could throw a party- that required money and an understanding family. She thought she could make friends by talking to them- but that was a non-starter. They appeared to want to mock her, not make casual conversation. Finally, she had an idea! Social media! She could write her social media handles on pieces of paper and post them in the lockers of her class. Everyone loved social media- Instagram, Facebook, Twitter, Snapchat. She was guaranteed to make friends that way!

Early the next day, Ava had received a message from Hannah. *Hi Ava, I would like to be your friend!* At last she had a friend that she could talk to when she had nothing to do! Ava began to spend a lot of time with Hannah, hanging out and going shopping. She loved the company and had found a kindred spirit- a new best friend. As a mark of her trust in Hannah, Ava gave her all the passwords for each of her social media accounts. Life was great again.

It was a few days later that Ava started receiving notifications on her social media accounts. Confused, she scrolled through her phone to find private messages and posts on her account that she simply hadn't made. A photograph of her had been posted on her Instagram account, calling her a bookworm and a nerd. Ava couldn't fathom it. In her inbox, there had been private messages exchanged with other girls in her class. Malicious messages. Sent *to* her and sent *from* her. It was news to Ava. She hadn't typed these messages. A couple of hours later, she found twenty-three notifications on Instagram. They were all comments about how Ava was so interested in her school work, how much thought she put into everything and how over the top they thought she was. Twenty three messages sent from twenty three different teenagers in her class. All sent within sixty seconds of one another. It felt co-ordinated. It felt planned. It felt targeted. The comments became increasingly nasty and vindictive as Ava scrolled down through them. Worse still, there were embarrassing pictures posted from when she was younger looking and extremely nerdy- glasses, braces and a *Team Edward* t-shirt. Twilight was no longer considered in vogue it seemed.

The cruel comments and embarrassing pictures carried on for days. She finally figured it out. Her new best friend. She'd given her all her passwords. She'd also posted her social media handles through the lockers of all her class.

The naivety. The betrayal. Ava began to feel withdrawn and unhappy with what was happening to her but she continued to keep it to herself. Until finally she became upset at home and told her Dad. She knew she had to tell him but she didn't want to. She didn't want any more trouble. She didn't want to be a loner again. She only wanted it to end. And quickly.

5

Love, it's unpredictable. Only some manage to find it and yet Edward and Ava did. The two who had been through war, heartbreak (and the subsequent alleviation of it) had finally tied the knot. It was the wedding of the century. Everyone was there, whether it was literally, in memory or in the womb of the bride. Yes, not only was there a ring upon her finger but an angel in the midst. A sweet baby girl was due and she would place the cherry on top of the ice-cream sundae, that was their dream-filled life. Enjoying every day as if it were their last, they thought life couldn't get any better. Then along came Aaron, the cherished boy who stood proud among his parents and sister as the family's only son. But things were to sour.

*   *   *   *   *   *

It all went black. A loud 'BANG!' emanated from downstairs. Then there were sirens. Sweet, sweet sirens that would drain the very colour from your cheeks in an instant, sending you crumbling to the floor in agony. It was Ava's mother. Visiting for her daughter's birthday, she had just gone downstairs for a glass of water when she had slipped on one of Aaron's toys. She tumbled down, down and down until the force of the impact with the concrete

20

floor finished her off. There had been no hope of saving her. No matter how hard the family cried; no matter how much they'd pleaded with the medics to do something, do anything, to try to save her, it was just too late. *Please! Take her! Fix her ! You must try!* A shrill scream echoed down the hallway. Tears streamed down Ava's cheeks, her arms tensely gripping the shoulders of one medic who looked on helplessly at the scene before him.

You must save her. Please, you must fix her.

Darling we must let them take her. There's nothing we can do for her now. Let God decide the rest, responded Edward.

God! God? What's he got to do with this? Why him? There is something we can do for her! We can help her! Ava insisted.

Sweetheart I know it's hard but we...

Oh, you know! Of course, you know! Edward, you have never had to go through this! You haven't seen the ambulance, the body bag. Edward fell silent. This was not the time to talk about the war.

Although that night harrowed Ava's heart, over time she gradually grew back into her normal self, seeing the world as a gift and not a cruel trick. And as pain turned to memories, spring became summer, months turned to years and like became love. Another family event bloomed. Celebrating the joining of Aaron and (his new wife) Lindsey, the whole family came round to their modest home to enjoy a peaceful and loving night. Passion danced around the fire that Edward had made and excitement arose as Ava presented the couple with a homemade cake and vases from her own wedding. Then it was time to dance.

Tension filled the room as the younger ones fumbled around, trying to find someone to dance with. But when it came to Edward and Ava, there would be no other choice but each other. They glided across the floor like they were on air, their eyes seeing only each other, as Beethoven's sweet melodies filled the room. Hand to hand they danced, oblivious to their surroundings, their thoughts and feelings only on one another. They walked the lines of their past, future and present all in one. True love- as fairytales say- yet theirs was no fantasy.

Minutes passed (yet it only felt like seconds) before they were torn apart by the constant whining of the guests, gasping with thirst as the wine had stopped flowing. Desperate to resume his loving state, Edward offered to refresh the supplies, leaving Ava stranded on the makeshift dance floor. The lit cake meanwhile, given as a gift, was left lying on the table. With nobody watching, the wind blew without care or consideration through the window. The fire had taken hold by the time everyone had noticed it.

The first thing Edward saw was the ambulance, then the smoke pouring out of all the windows in sight. The sound was deafening as fire engines stood lined like brutish soldiers, trying to put a stop to the devilish magic that consumed the humble family home. Edward was left, watching the flames ravage the house. Not everyone had made it out. His beloved Ava was gone. Edward's world was plunged into darkness.

Uncertain of what to do and seeking solace in his memories, Edward wrote to her. And not just once. He faithfully placed each of his letters to Ava under a floorboard beneath his bed.

My Dearest Ava ,

I can't believe you're gone. I thought we were destined to grow old together. Watching you leave was terrible. My heart is filled with sadness. My only comfort is that you will soon find happiness again and you know that I am always going to be here for you. I miss you so much and life isn't life without you. We will see each other soon though, I can feel it.

A whole new life awaits you and soon everyone will know how amazing you are. I know that everything feels empty right now and you feel like you're in hell, but you have more love in your little finger than some people possess in their whole body. No matter where you are, no matter where you go, I will always be with you. If people cannot see the beauty within you then they're not worth it.

Now you must rest and I know that the angels will look out for you. Remember that. I wish I could be there with you. I wish I'd never left you so that I could help you get through this. The pain won't last my dear but the guilt and remorse I feel will take me to my grave.

You must stay strong my love, for the world isn't ready to let you go yet and nor am I. Show them who they should be adoring or else they will never know any different. I love you and I'm sure that others will too. Stay strong. You are more than you will ever know to me. I will forever be buried in guilt and love,

Edward

x

6

Dear Ava,

There isn't a day that goes by without me thinking of you. I cannot bear being apart from you anymore. The only thing that keeps me going is the thought of your beautiful face. Just thinking about you and knowing that I can still speak to you brightens my day. Words cannot describe how much I miss you.

Yours always,

Edward
x

It was dark by the time Ava stepped through the door. Summer turns to autumn quickly. Light fades to dark. She trudged up the stairs after another disappointing day at school. She wished she was back home. Back with Kirsten, Paula, Jill, Katy and Sophie. Back in her old room. Back with *Mum*, back when it was Mum *and* Dad. Back in her old life.

Entering her room, she threw her satchel onto the floor. She watched it slide across the exposed floorboards, stopping at the foot of the bed. She examined the buckles from a distance. One was undone. But her eyeline was drawn to something unusual immediately below her bed. The floorboards. One of them appeared raised. Dislodged. Out of place. Even from a distance, she could see that it wasn't right. Leaning down, she reached under the bed to slot the loose board back into place. That's when she saw it. White. Red. Paper. Wrapped in a bow. Leaning further forward, a sheet of paper slid between her fingers. She delicately removed it, handling it like it was relic from the tomb of some forgotten Pharoah. Unwrapping the red bow, her eyes scanned the page. She noticed that it was a letter. Addressed to her. From a man she'd never heard of. Edward. There was only one Edward she knew of. A boy at her new school. But why would he write to her? How did he know where she lived? How would he be able to place the letter under a floorboard in her room? She dismissed the notion immediately.

Try as she might, for an hour, Ava couldn't stop thinking about the letter she had found under her bed. The name Edward was drowning her thoughts. Trying to forget it, she went to bed. But when she woke up in the morning she felt drenched in an anxious sweat as all night she was worried what her new *'friends'* might have to say about it. Ava decided she would tell Jenny and Angela. What was the worst that could happen?

She didn't have to wait long to find out. When she arrived at school, she told them what had happened. She realised how ludicrous it sounded as she heard herself say it aloud. But it was true. Undeniably true. Lost in her thoughts and oblivious to her immediate surroundings, more heard the fantastical tale than Ava had intended to. As soon as she mentioned Edward Middleton, her fate was sealed. The baying crowd erupted in hysterical laughter. *Ava likes Ed.* She was mocked and accused. Even her so called *'friends'* joined in. She ran off, bitterly upset.

There was no respite for days. Everywhere she went, Ava was teased and ridiculed. She couldn't tell her Dad. He was always working to make ends meet. School dramas, boys, and friendships had always been Mum's area. Ava dreaded going to school.

The next morning, she walked to school alone. As she went to open her locker, a tonne of letters fell out with ED ♥written all over them. Realising she was the victim of a prank, Ava burst into tears. She went to see the school nurse, telling her she was ill and wanted to go home. Sitting there in the school infirmary, Ava finally decided that she would write back. She needed someone to confide in and Ed was clearly someone who valued her. On Saturday morning she wrote her reply.

Hi Edward,

I'm so glad to have received your letter. It's not what I thought it would be like here. I thought I'd be okay being away from those that loved me. But I'm not. I've not been here that long. I suppose I should give it more of a chance. I'm sorry for just pouring out these words but I feel like I can talk to you. Thank you for the lovely bow you wrapped the letter in. My favourite colour too. It's beautiful.

Love,

Ava.

x

7

An alarm rang, startling Edward. He realised he had been daydreaming. His mind had wandered to days gone by. Memories of day trips to Blackpool with his wife and friends; deckchairs, dandelion and burdock, sticks of rock- it all felt so real.

The faint smell of disinfectant and road noise rumbling in the distance brought him back to the reality of Broadoak Nursing Home. The four walls he had called home for the last year had surrounded him since he took a tumble outside his house. His son, Aaron, had deemed him unable to cope on his own, so this was his reality now. The same armchair, the same awful food, the same five films on repeat. Oh to be somewhere but here.

Edward sighed and slowly got up off his bed. Reaching down for his old comfy slippers, he noticed something was different. Under the pressure of his weight, the floorboard shifted and creaked with a yawn. His valuables! Edward, like many people his age, had a healthy mistrust of banks and chose to keep his pension and other treasures under the floorboards. Had he been robbed? He felt sick as he slowly moved the rug then the loose board. He expected the worst. To his surprise, his money tin and the letters from his beloved wife Ava were still there. The letters were decades old and were Edward's most treasured possessions. The paper was tattered and torn, but the words gave him comfort. To his great surprise, however, a crisp white envelope sat peacocking proudly at the top of the bundle. How had it got there? Surely no one had broken into his room and left him a note to say they had done so? His hand trembled as he pondered whether or not to open it. He sat for what seemed like an age staring at the letter, questions floating around in his head. Edward shuffled over to the sideboard and removed a silver paper knife, which was a present for 25 years of service as an employee. With a flick of the wrist, the envelope was opened and he began to read the letter.

He sat and read the letter three times. Bewildered, he asked himself how it could be. How could Ava be writing to him? Was it really her? Or was someone at the nursing home misguidedly trying to comfort a grieving old man. Edward was no fool. Only for Ava. And he knew that the staff knew it too. He pondered for many hours, trying to think of ways it could be his deceased wife Ava. Talking to him. From beyond the grave. He knew it couldn't be. But he desperately wanted to believe it. Maybe he had finally lost his marbles. His son was always joking that it would happen. Was it one of his friends? Was he asleep and dreaming? He decided it couldn't be a dream as the tea was too unpleasant- even for a nightmare! He considered it again. What if it was really her? He missed her so much.

How he had prayed for this, to have one last conversation with her. There was so much he wanted to say.

Dazed and confused, Edward decided it was finally time to get dressed. He settled on dark brown trousers and a beige jumper, which was pretty much his uniform nowadays. He stepped into his favourite pair of loafers, grabbed his walking stick and gingerly made his way down the stairs clutching the letter. Halfway down the dimly lit corridor, a nursing assistant opened the curtains letting the morning sun flood into the building. Edward's eyes struggled to focus in the blinding light. *Miss, Miss can you help me?* The assistant stared in his general direction. *Go through to the breakfast room Ed; plenty of toast this morning.* Edward was confused by the reply. She was clearly not listening. He persisted with more force, *No, no I have a letter. Do you know anything about it?* He waited anxiously for her response, hanging on every word she said. *No luv, musta come in this mornin's post.*

Still no closer to finding out who wrote the letter, Edward decided to interrupt the news bulletin to ask Edith about the letter. *I received a strange letter today, do you know anything about it?* He passed Edith her reading glasses and she proceeded to read the letter. *I have no idea, luv. Strange one that, must be from your wife, Ava.*

That night after supper, Edward started his nightly routine. He folded his clothes, had a wash, brushed his teeth and settled in for the night. He said his nightly prayers and asked for Ava to show him a sign that the letter was from her. *Ava, I miss you so much. I hope you are well. I got a letter today. I think it's from you, I hope it is from you. Please show me a sign.*

Edward found it difficult to get to sleep over the road noise so listened to the wireless. Tuning in, the first sound he heard was their wedding song. It all came flooding back. The dress. The smile. The first dance. The girl. Ava. In his mind it was as clear a sign as there could be. At that moment he decided he would respond to Ava's letter. It was rude to look a gift horse in the mouth. He was going to accept it and be grateful.

The letter swirled around in his head most of the night. Vivid dreams jolted him awake. That aching feeling of loss for his childhood sweetheart had never left him since her passing. *Oh Ava* he thought as the sunlight peeped through the dark blue curtains of his room. He got up and took out his old fountain pen from his side table and the writing paper from the drawer. He proceeded to write.

My Darling Ava,

It feels like such a terribly long time since I last wrote to you. I am overwhelmed that I received your letter. Words cannot express how your letter has my heart dancing with joy. No letter of yours has ever been more welcome and if only you could see how happy I am. Is it really you?

Our song came on the radio last night. I saw it as sign you are watching over me. I talk to your picture most days and can still hear your laughter in the hallways. I have so many questions and so much I want to say. Have my prayers really been answered?

I miss you. Every time I watch a film ,I can't ask your opinion. Every time I See your favourite flower bloom outside my window, I think of you. I miss you most at night. I still remember all those very many wonderful years we had together. I feel so alone without you .I have had no one to be by my side since you left me and no one to share anything with. I wish you were still here.

I will pray you write back.

All my love,

Edward

8

That same night, Ava had quite a strange dream, a dream that involved the man himself- Edward. It all began with her waking up and receiving a reply. However this reply was different compared with all the previous letters she had received.

Dear Ava,

I just want to tell you . . . how much of a loser you are! You should've seen the look on the our faces when we found out you actually replied to Edward's - my- letter. Did you really think someone actually wanted to be your 'friend'? Oh, I don't know what kind of planet you're living on because on everyone else's planet you're such a loner, a dork and, as some say, a goody two shoes! You're such a weird person.

Edward

Traumatised by the letter, her adrenalin woke her up earlier than usual. Glancing at the floorboard, she caught sight of the white of yet another letter. The moment she slid it out from under the floorboard she started to wonder if her dream was reality: if the letter was written by a person in her school, if everyone really thought about her in that kind of way. Reading the letter, she was relieved that her dream wasn't real, the letter was just one of his usual ones. However, how could she be sure? Maybe they were writing all of the letters behind her back? Maybe they were waiting for the right time to humiliate her in front of the whole school? Just to be sure, she decided to investigate to find out whether or not someone from school was writing the letters as a prank.

Seconds before leaving the house, Ava gathered up the collection of letters as evidence. Firstly, she asked at reception to see *exactly* how many Edwards attended the school- had she missed someone? She *still* didn't trust herself. As predicted, there were several Edwards. During the break Ava tracked them down- one by one. They looked completely oblivious when confronted with the letters- even Ava could see that. Nearing the end of break, she approached the final Edward on her list. She had expected him to be with a group of people but to her surprise he was on his own, his thick lensed glasses partially hidden behind the book he was reading. Clenching the letters in one hand, she grabbed Edward, pushing him up against the nearest wall; she shoved the letters in front of his face and questioned him. *Do you recognise these? Who do you think you are trying to pretend to be this wonderful person? Why are you doing this to me, humiliating me in front of everyone?* The confused expression on his face told her he had nothing to do with it; he was innocent. Nevertheless, she carried on until he finally snapped back, *W ... what are you doing to me. I'm innocent. I really don't know what you are talking about. Stop!* Ava suddenly froze and saw that she was surrounded by a huge audience, not for the first time this week. She felt their glares burning her skin, telling her that she didn't belong there. She ran into the toilets, crying. She felt just as humiliated as she probably would have, had those letters *actually* been written by him

In class, the same type of thing happened again; everyone stepped away from her when she tried to go near them. The teacher didn't speak to her for the whole day. She knew this wasn't her fault. How could *she know* they were innocent, the amount of torturous things they did to her? She thought about how much everyone hated her, how they all looked at her, despising her. She couldn't be in the same room with people who didn't want her there, people who thought she was mad. She ran once again to the bathroom and didn't want to come out. She didn't want to be in a place where people thought she was crazy and had issues.

Leaving the bathroom, Ava went back into the classroom. As she entered the room, all eyes were on her yet again. The students held their noses and started making trumping noises. She sat down in embarrassment and waited for the final minutes of the school day to pass her by. It felt like an hour later when finally the bell went and she raced past the gates until she was out of sight of everyone. Whilst she was running, people pointed and talked about her to their parents- about what she had done to Edward and how crazy she was. She took the longest way home that day as she didn't want anyone to see her. It took her over forty minutes instead of her usual twenty.

Concerned, her dad rang her, yelling at her from the other end of the phone, not even thinking to ask her if she needed a lift home or even if she was okay. *Ava, come home now, you stupid girl.* He ranted at her for another five minutes. Tears streamed down Ava's face, her whole body trembling. She truly felt that her dad didn't care for her. Deep inside she knew he loved her despite him never really managing to show it. Well, at least not since Mum died. She really wanted to tell someone about Edward, someone she could trust. Her dad seemed like her only option. Ava thought she'd give him another chance to prove he loved her. She would tell him about the letter.

After tea, she found Dad, half asleep on the sofa. She tapped him on the back. He was half asleep when he responded. *What is it now, Ava?* Ava got the message. She knew it was pretty pointless telling him about Edward, about the letters. She knew he wouldn't listen and didn't really care. Nevertheless, she had to do it; she had to tell someone. Plucking up the courage, she approached him again. *Dad, I erm just well, kind of wanted to tell you about something.* He yawned his mouth slowly open as if he was about to speak but stopped himself and let Ava carry on. Filled with hope (and happiness that he may have changed) she carried on. *Well, like I mentioned before, I wanted to speak to you about something and I promise it's real.* She held up one of Edward's letters and handed it over to her Dad. A dichotomy of emotions, she was at once both terrified at what he would say and proud of herself for having unburdened her dark secret.

Dad scanned the letters before looking at her, his burrow frowning and his eyes narrowing. Ava was just about to explain about the letters when he spoke. *You are such a cheeky rascal, Ava Jane Davis, thinking I would fall for this dumb prank of yours. I even thought you were going to talk about something intelligent for once, something normal- maybe tell me about your day for a change. Instead, you're once again messing with my head. Haven't we had enough of this nonsense since your Mum died?* Ava was just about to speak when he continued. *What? What is it now? Because I don't have a clue what you are going to say anymore or what you're thinking!* Ava stared at him, in shock that he could be so cold. To be so cold to mention Mum in that way. Ava told him it didn't matter.

She ran upstairs and wondered if everyone thought of her as a timewasting crazy girl. The only person that she felt understood and listened to what she had to say was Edward. *Her Edward.* She didn't even know if he was real, but she was sure that he was the only person she could turn to right now. She decided to reply to his letter.

Dear Edward,

I'm really shocked right now because this - whatever this is - might actually be real. I embarrassed myself in front of everyone so I could find out - for sure- if it was actually you. Thank you for finding me, for reaching out to me because right now I feel like you are the only one that actually understands me. Here, in this unfamiliar place, I don't know anyone. But knowing that you're thinking of me - that you continue to think of me - brings enormous comfort. I hope we can keep in touch. I've no idea how you are managing to reach me with your letters but they are the only thing that makes me smile these days.

Yours,

Ava

x

9

It had only just been dinner. Edward slowly and carefully lifted his walking stick and made his way back to his room. As he reached for his glasses, he noticed the broken floorboard -where he had been storing all his letters to his late wife Ava- had been disturbed. *Those disrespectful nurses peeping at my private property, I'll have them for that!* Stubbornly, he lifted up the floorboard. He paused for a moment. Was it? Could it be? Another letter from Ava. Wrapped beautifully in a rich, maroon-coloured bow. Edward staggered to his bed and gently opened the letter. His eyes filling with tears, he began to read. *Ava, you're here ...but I thought you'd gone.* At that moment, he burst into tears.

After he had finally stopped crying, and his eyes were no longer bloodshot, Edward gently kissed the letter - as if it were Ava herself. As he did so, his attention was drawn to the bow once again. Its deep, rich colour and messy, frayed ends. It brought back memories of Ava, of how she would wrap letters or gifts in rich, maroon bows and kiss them as she sent them away to her friends and family. Edward tossed the bow from one hand to another- wondering how his late wife could be contacting him- when he spotted the initials sewed into the bow. 'AW' - Ava White. It was Ava's bow after all.

No, no. It can't be! It just couldn't! Despite his earlier acceptance that it was Ava, Edward knew it couldn't be. He'd went along with it. Willingly fooled. Like a child at a magic show. How could Ava be writing back to him? He had missed her and never stopped grieving for her! *It's, it's not possible, Edward! For goodness sake, she is dead!* He fell silent. It was true- his only love was dead. Or was she? Thoughts raced through Edward's mind; no-one could have Ava's bow, but Ava. But how could Ava have the bow in heaven? If Ava didn't have the bow, who did? Edward lay down and rested his head upon the pillow- yet he couldn't sleep. He'd taken his medication and brushed his teeth- what else was there left to do? He knew that the real reason he couldn't sleep was Ava. He needed answers. And he needed them now.

The next morning, after breakfast and a good-old game of chess, Edward headed for the charity shop. He had remembered how the care home staff had took some of Ava's belongings away, including her bow. Rushing down the lively streets, he soon found himself where many of Ava's belongings went. He knew for sure that it was the right place because some of Ava's clothes were still there. He searched and searched for the bow but couldn't find it anywhere. It must have been sold, but to who? Could Ava have retrieved the bow? Whoever bought the bow knew Edward and was writing to him now.

After lunch, and a little backgammon, Edward wrote back to 'Ava'. He prepared his fountain pen and paper. But to begin with, he couldn't find the words. Nothing seemed right. Nothing seemed good enough. He didn't dare ask his carers to help him. He didn't want them to know; if they found out he was writing love letters to his deceased wife- who knows what they may do! After a while, Edward settled on an opening sentence and began to write.

Dear Ava,

I have just received your latest letter and I must ask- how did you get the bow? The staff at my nursing-home took some of your belongings away when you left us and gave them to the local charity shop. I checked back there just this morning, however, and the bow wasn't there anymore. Did you really come back? Are you able to walk these streets once again? How did you get the bow?

I know we have both lost someone but, even though we're apart, I am still always by your side. And I know you'll always be by my side too. We have remained together through thick and thin and we're ready to face any storm that faces us.

So, how are things where you are? How are you coping with the change? Is it hard up there? Or is life a breeze? I would have thought that away from this awful place would be peaceful. Is it all people dream it is? Have you met anyone we know? Have you made new friends? Are you being treated well?

I can't believe we've found each other. I can't

believe my luck. I absolutely adore your letters. I can't wait to speak to you again.

All my love,

Edward

x

10

Dear Edward,

I need you here with me; no one could be you, I swear. Since I've been here my whole life has turned upside down. Without any real friends, I just can't cope! I need you here with me. Other than you, I have no-one to confide in. And the bow- I didn't find the bow; it found me. As soon as I laid my eyes on it, I knew. I knew it was meant for me. Now that I've got the bow, I can use it as a reminder of you. When I'm feeling down, I can hold the bow close and be happy once more.

You are the only thing that makes me feel elated; not the sun, not the stars, not being around other people. Your kind words and letters are what keep me wanting to stay and wait for wherever life will take me next. Take us next. Because, believe it or not, in spite of my words, I love life. Well, I loved life.

Since I've moved on, every aspect of my life is hellish- not just because it is so different here but because I feel like I'm invisible. People walk past me like they can't see me; like I don't exist. It's like I don't matter. It makes me feel so upset. It's not all it's cracked up to be here- it's even worse than it is in the big bad world out there. People gossip and spread rumours; they say terrible things. About me. To me. I thought it'd be different here. Peaceful. A chance to see the bigger picture.

And then there's you. Throughout all this, there's always you. I wish I was back home; I used to have people who cared for me and wanted to keep me safe from all the hurt. But I had to leave. It was my time to go. If I had had any choice, I never would have left. I miss that love and warmth. I felt safe - like I always have done with you. I know you would have stopped it if you could. But you can't. It all happened so suddenly. And then I was here. It's just not what I expected. I don't know what I expected to be honest. But it wasn't this. I'm so glad we've connected again- your letters help take away the pain. I hope you're feeling fine and know how special you are to me. I hope my letters bring you some comfort and that you can enjoy life even though I'm not there.

You're special, Edward. I've sensed a deep sadness in your previous letters. You've been through darker times than this. You'll feel whole again. I'll help you. We'll help each other. Hang on in there. And thank you for being you.

Love from,
Ava

XX

11

Edward woke as soon as the light seeped through a crack in his curtains. He tiptoed out of bed trying not to make a sound; it was as if he had a sixth sense, as if he knew that the letter awaited him underneath the floorboard. Walking with a slight limp, Edward ventured to the raised board jutting out from the floor, and got on his knees to read the letter that lay before him. The floorboard was carefully lifted by his shaking hand. Having read it, he put the letter back and struggled onto his feet with the help of his bed.

In a daze, he plodded slowly along the corridor to the lounge and checked the news. *Nothing new; same old, same old,* he muttered to himself. Turning away from the screen, something caught his eye. A face on the screen. It couldn't be. It wasn't. He was mistaken. Yet again. He'd been doing it since the death of his wife. Seeing her everywhere. Seeing her *name* everywhere. But it had intensified since he'd been receiving her letters. Everything had Ava written all over it. It was as if the letters had given him hope, somehow, that she was still alive, somewhere. But she couldn't be, could she?

All the thinking had made Edward tired. He curled up in a ball on the sofa and settled down to rest his eyes and his thoughts. However, he was soon woken by Margaret doing her rounds with the meds. *Hello Edward, how are you today?* Her voice was always filled with great enthusiasm. *Fine, thank you,* came his startled reply. Margaret moved closer and leaned down to speak to him. *Ready for your meds?* she asked sweetly. Edward replied with a less than enthusiastic grunt. Taking his tablets from Margaret, he quickly swallowed them, one after another, until all four were gone. Margaret said her goodbyes and walked off with her trolley to the next room. Edward shut his eyes and drifted off into a deep sleep. He was back with her. Dreaming of the happy times he'd shared with his dear wife. The trip to Blackpool in '37. The wind in her hair on the beach. The donkey rides and the long walks.

Edward woke to see he had been asleep for over two hours. Hunger harried him. But he didn't want to move. He often felt like this when he woke. The realisation that he was alone- without *her*- was often too great in the first few moments after sleep. Edward felt he was becoming more secluded as each day passed. Ava's letters made him feel young and kept his spirits high, but they did nothing to help him socialise with the other pensioners. One of the nurses eventually persuaded him to accompany her to the dining room where she gave him some toast and coffee. Edward ate, lost in deep thought; thoughts about his next letter to Ava. His mind was racing, thoughts piercing his mind.

Julie, the kitchen supervisor, cleared away Edward's plate and cup whilst he mentally prepared his reply to Ava. Edward shuffled along the corridor at a much quicker pace than he had come down them hours before. The thought of writing to his dear wife gave him a keen sense of purpose. He changed his clothes, brushed his teeth and put some aftershave on; Ava's favourite. He was ready to begin his reply. He sat at his desk eagerly searching for his best pen. After a moment of thought he began.

My Dearest Ava,

I still cannot believe you found the bow. It's so beautiful and brings back so many happy memories. My heart warms when I read your letters. They take me back to the old days. I dreamed about you last night. Our trip to Blackpool in 1937. We were there again. I got to relive it all and it was magical. I know you were there with me. Just being near you, just sensing you are here makes me feel young again.

Yours always,

Edward
xx

Having put his reply under the floorboard, Edward wandered back off to the lounge for Book Club. Alice, Michael, Peggy, Albert and Helen were all there. Helen, the leader of the book club, cleared her throat and began. *Where are we all up to with the book?* she asked curiously. They were all about to start chapter five. Except Edward. He had completed the whole book from front to back. It meant he could devote himself to reading Ava's favourite novel, *Wuthering Heights*. He was already a good quarter of the way through. Being the modest, sweet man that he was, Edward didn't boast about having finishing the novel. He just sat and politely gave his opinions on what had happened in the first four chapters. He was mindful not to disclose any further details which could ruin it for the rest of the group.

Once the meeting was over, Edward said his goodbyes to his friends and went back to reading about Heathcliff and Catherine. Every page he turned reminded him of Ava, the scent of her sweet perfume catching his nose with every turn of a page. A tear waltzed slowly and elegantly down his cheek and onto the book. The tear on the page made him feel like they were together again. The words were Ava. The tear was Edward. It was as if by magic. A chain reaction had been set in motion. Edward smiled and within a split second, one whole side of his body drooped. He tried to call her. *Ava, Ava let me be with you!* But he could hear his words slur as they flopped from his mouth.

Edward heard a voice. A familiar one. It was Ava. His dear wife. Now he was sure. More sure than ever. It was time for him to be reunited with her. The two beautiful souls sealed the great moment with a kiss as Edward's eyes shut for the final time. They were together again. Edward and Ava. Together again in love and at peace.

When he was laid to rest the following week, Edward was buried next to his beloved Ava. The eulogy spoke of how they were together again. It was more accurate than the speaker could ever have hoped. For they were together. Together again, forever.

12

After hours of waiting, Ava arrived home after experiencing yet another tormenting day at school. Coming home was the only thing she actually looked forward to; it meant another letter from this mystery man.

Her eyes – two bright sapphires- gleamed with joy as she darted to her room. Edging towards the floorboard, her face lit up as she saw she had received yet another reply; her fingers started to tremble and, as her finger sliced open the white paper, a sudden warm, cosy feeling hit her heart. She was delighted to hear that her letters made him feel young and cared for once again- his letters made her feel a similar way. Furthermore, she was pleased that they both helped each other through the day! Several minutes later, she placed the letter on top of her previous ones in a wooden drawer. Strangely, she couldn't help thinking about who this person *really* was. As usual she decided to write a reply.

Dear Edward,

Thank you so much for replying; as you know, your words mean a lot to me. I feel as though you're the only person that I can really talk to. I'm so glad that my letters make you feel young and cared-for again because yours actually make me feel a similar sort of way. They are the only things that keep me happy. You've really helped me through tough times. It occurred to me today that we have been talking for weeks and, while I know you're a nice person, I don't really know who you are. I was wondering - after reading your beautiful letter-if it would be possible for you to send me a photograph; just so I have an idea of who you are, that's all. I know I have already mentioned this, but I just want to make sure you know that your letters make me feel special and I appreciate you taking the time to write them. I'm hopeful that you'll keep replying because you really do shine light upon my darkest of days.

Love from
Ava

Xx

After sealing shut the envelope, she gently slid the rectangular paper under the floorboard hoping that in the next day or so she would get a reply. Several hours later, after arriving upstairs Ava took a quick glimpse at the floor board then tucked herself into bed as normal. The next day, she awoke and peered round her bed to see if a letter was there; however, to her surprise, there wasn't so she presumed it might be there when she arrived home from school, having endured hell.

On the bus, Ava started to find it odd that her letter hadn't been delivered in the morning. She thought she was being rather daft and impatient, that maybe he didn't have time to write one. After numerous hours, Ava arrived back home. Upon opening her bedroom door, she was smothered by a wave of pure shock- there was still no letter. Checking the floorboard inside and out, there was no sign of one. Distraught, she went to her bed, falling straight to sleep. She hoped that in the morning a letter would be waiting for her, waiting to be read.

Awaking rather early after an uneasy night's sleep, she took a glimpse at her floorboard and once again found that there wasn't a letter waiting to be read. Taking a second look, she knew for certain it wasn't there. A third check confirmed it. When she returned home from school, there was still no letter. Ava didn't know how to feel. How could a stranger turn her world upside down? How could he save her only to abandon her? Several days past without any joy: no letter in the morning, no delivery in the evening.

After ten long days, Ava began to feel different- the purple patch of happiness which she had found in her heart had become the depths of despair and she started to feel pathetic. She had believed that Edward was real, believed he had actually liked her, believed he loved her letters.

Later that evening, she didn't go to see if there was a letter under the floorboard because she knew there wouldn't be; she could no longer bear the disappointment. Climbing wearily into bed, she noticed something under the floorboard. Thinking she was imagining things, she went back to bed. One hour later, her head pondering with thoughts, she was still wide awake. Deep down she knew Edward would reply. She felt it. She knew there was something there. Eventually deciding to get up, she peered over her bed at the floorboard underneath. There! She saw it. A glimmer of white. Gazing back at her. Locking eyes with her. Reaching out for it, an overwhelming feeling of excitement hit her heart once again.

27 September 1965

Dear Ava,

You probably don't know who I am so allow me to introduce myself. My name is Margaret and I am an attendant from your beloved Edward's nursing home. You're probably perplexed as to why I'm writing and to be honest I don't want to be the one to say this. However, our much-loved darling Edward has now made his way to heaven. I am truly devastated to be the one to announce this dreadful, distressing news.

I would just like to tell you that he had a lovely last week in our nursing home. I know he would have wished to spend his last week with you. He'd have moved heaven and Earth to make it happen, if he could. He told me specifically to tell you that he will try his hardest to find you. He frequently mentioned how your letters made his life worth living because, at one point, he had all but given up on the very thought of it.

Your letters changed everything. Personally, I couldn't believe the change in the man since he started receiving them. He was a man re-born, reinvigorated. We struggled to believe that he was speaking with you and for that I feel ashamed. He took such care in keeping his letters to you bound in this beautiful bow. He called them his 'Prayers' to Ava. He said that your letters had answered all his prayers and he

55

wanted his to answer yours.

Words cannot express how truly sorry I am for this loss and devastation.

Yours Faithfully,
Margaret

Reading the letter, Ava couldn't believe what she saw. She read the piece of paper again to make sure she wasn't imagining things. This couldn't be true. How could it possibly be true? She decided that she was dreaming; she believed that desperation had invaded her sleep. However a part of her mind knew that she was wrong, she knew this was real.

Heading to the bathroom, she splashed water over her face. Nothing happened. She slapped her face. Nothing happened. She wasn't dreaming... this was reality. It was true. The letter was from the year 1965. She had been talking to the past- to a ghost. Edward- the man who had made her feel so alive- was in fact, dead. A chill ran down her spine leaving her feeling paralysed. Frozen to the spot, she couldn't move until the wave of bewilderment passed her by. Calming herself down, she couldn't visualise herself talking to the past. How could she? It was supernatural; it was considered impossible. Until now! Could she tell anyone? No, they wouldn't believe her; they would think she was delusional and probably send her to a psychiatric hospital. This bizarre part of her life would have to remain a mammoth secret.

ABOUT THE AUTHORS

Writing a short novel is no small feat. To do so, at the tender age of ten or eleven is all the more remarkable. Our children showed incredible empathy, compassion and resilience in creating the characters and the plot of this story. We are incredibly proud of them and are certain that they will look back on this experience with incredible fondness.

OTHER STORIES BY
JAMES BRINDLEY COMMUNITY PRIMARY
SCHOOL:

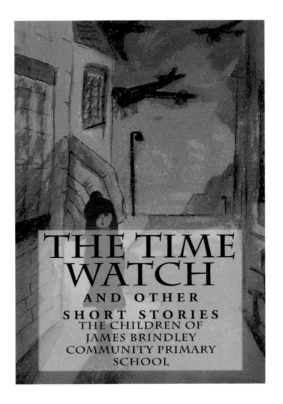

Superheroes, secrets, and villainous teachers- this
is the second volume of short stories by the
children of James Brindley Community Primary
School. From aliens to animals, volcanoes to ghosts,
you're guaranteed to be entertained!

Available at Amazon.co.uk

OTHER STORIES BY
JAMES BRINDLEY COMMUNITY PRIMARY
SCHOOL:

I know that look. I've seen it a million times before.
Sympathy. Pity. Sadness. Mum's crying. She's angled her
face away from me to try to conceal it. But I'm not daft-
I know when she's crying. She's been doing it a lot lately.

*Charlie knows something is wrong. But what if something
is so badly broken that it cannot be fixed?*

Available at Amazon.co.uk

OTHER STORIES BY
JAMES BRINDLEY COMMUNITY PRIMARY
SCHOOL:

From monsters to flying burgers, ghosts to midnight elephants, the stories in this book have been written simply for pleasure. Pleasure for the writer, the parent, the teacher, the reader.

Available at Amazon.co.uk

Printed in Great Britain
by Amazon